Farmer Bill

Matthew Fernandes

Key Porter Kids

For Mom and Dad

National Library of Canada Cataloguing in Publication Data

Fernandes, Matthew
    Farmer Bill

ISBN 1-55263-382-9

I. Title

PS 8561.E75967F37 2001   jC813'.6   C2001-901279-9
PZ.F363Fa 2001

THE CANADA COUNCIL | LE CONSEIL DES ARTS
FOR THE ARTS | DU CANADA
SINCE 1957 | DEPUIS 1957

ONTARIO ARTS COUNCIL
CONSEIL DES ARTS DE L'ONTARIO

The publisher gratefully acknowledges the support of the Canada Council for the Arts and the Ontario Arts Council for its publishing program.

We acknowledge the financial support of the Government of Canada through the Book Publishing Industry Development Program (BPIDP) for our publishing activities.

Key Porter kids
is an imprint of
Key Porter Books Limited
70 The Esplanade
Toronto, Ontario
Canada M5E 1R2

www.keyporter.com

Design: Patricia Cavazzini

Printed and bound in Singapore

01 02 03 04 05 06 6 5 4 3 2 1

Farmer Bill

C/ 2125 O88
O7104

As the morning sun peeked over the hills, the rooster crowed a mighty crow, waking Farmer Bill from his dreams.

Every day began this way, and with this, Farmer Bill was happy.

After breakfast, Farmer Bill went out to feed the chickens. He collected the eggs and piled them high in his sturdy straw basket.
With this, he was happy.

Then, Farmer Bill went off to milk the cows.
He filled the tin buckets with creamy white milk.
With this, too, he was happy.

In the afternoon, Farmer Bill went out to shear the sheep. He piled their woolly coats into burlap bags. And with this, he was happy.

And when all the chores were done,
Farmer Bill and Mrs. Bill watched the
sun go down behind the hill.

VROOM! SCREECH!

One day, Little Bill came to visit from the city. Little Bill arrived in a big, flashy car. It had been some time since they'd seen their son, and this was a wonderful surprise.

Little Bill hugged Mrs. Bill and Farmer Bill and told them about life in the big city. They stayed up talking half the night.

The very next morning at the crack of dawn,
just like every other morning at the crack of dawn,
the rooster crowed a mighty crow.

Little Bill moaned, "What a horrible way to start the day!"

He crawled out of bed, drove into town, and came back with a clock radio.

"Here!" he said to Farmer Bill. "Now you can wake up to music. Nobody wakes up to roosters anymore. Get with the times, Dad!"

"Well ... alright," said Farmer Bill.
"Uh oh," said Mrs. Bill.

Upon hearing the news that he had been replaced, the rooster packed his bag and went to stay with his Aunt Matilda.

The very next day, Little Bill burst into the hen house with a big surprise.

"It's called the Egg-O-Matic!" he cried. "This marvelous machine makes eggs twice as fast as those old hens. And the eggs are three times bigger. Think of all the time you'll save!"

"Well ... alright," said Farmer Bill.
"Uh oh," said Mrs. Bill.

Upon hearing the news that they had been replaced, the chickens went off to live by the sea.

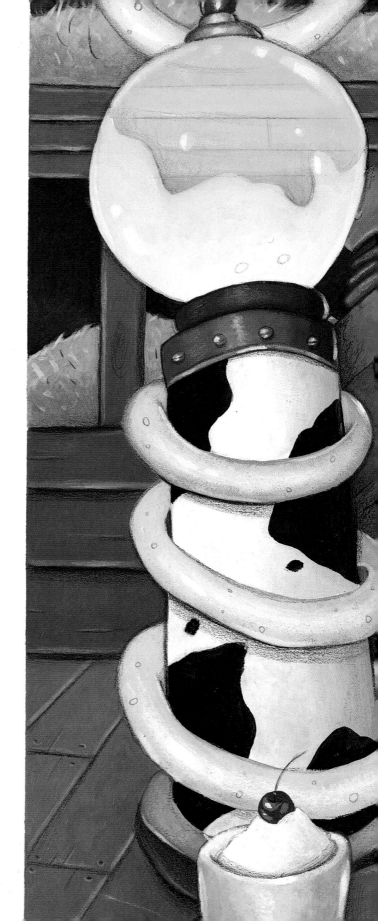

Several days later, Little Bill
ran into the barn with yet
another surprise.
"It's called the Amazing
Milk Maker!" he cried.
"It makes three times
the milk as those
old-fashioned cows,
and you don't have
to lift a finger.
Imagine all the time
you'll save!"

"Well ... alright," said Farmer Bill.
"Uh oh" said Mrs. Bill.

Upon hearing the news that they had been replaced, the cows left the farm to take up golf.

Things began to move pretty quickly on the farm: so many machines, so many changes. And (as Farmer Bill was about to discover) it wasn't over yet.

"It's called the Wondrous Wooly Weaver!" cried Little Bill.
"It makes wool four times faster, in six different colors, and you don't need any sheep! Imagine the time you'll save now!"

Farmer Bill scratched his head.
"Uh-oh," said Mrs. Bill.

Upon hearing the news that they had been replaced, the sheep left the farm to go skiing in the mountains.

Everything seemed to be taken care of, so Little Bill kissed his parents goodbye and returned to the city.

Months went by.

The radio turned itself on and off.

The Egg-O-Matic made twice as many eggs.

The Amazing Milk Maker made three times the milk.

The Wondrous Wooly Weaver made four times the wool in six different colors.

One day Little Bill phoned, "Isn't it great?" he asked. "Now you're the most successful farmer in the world! Thanks to technology, you finally have time to relax and be happy!"

But even though the farm produced twice as many eggs, three times the milk, and four times the wool (in six different colors), Farmer Bill wasn't happy.

He decided to take up painting to pass away the time.

He painted cows with baby calves. He painted sheep with baby lambs. He painted roosters. He painted hens. When he ran out of paper, he painted on the walls. He painted on the furniture. He even painted on the eggs.

One day, when there was nothing left in the house that wasn't painted, he put down his brushes and sighed. "I'm not Painter Bill. I'm Farmer Bill. I don't want to be the greatest farmer in the world. I want to be me. And I don't like these machines. Please, take them away."

Mrs. Bill was thoughtful. She'd never seen her husband so sad before.

The very next morning she sent letters to all the animals.

"**W**e miss you," she wrote.
"Please come home."

And do you know what?
They did.

And with this, Farmer
Bill was happy.